The Cellist's Notebook

Kittie Lambton

London | New York

Published by Clink Street Publishing 2019

Copyright © 2019

First edition.

The author asserts the moral right under the Copyright, Designs and
Patents Act 1988 to be identified as the author of this work.

All rights reserved. No part of this publication may be reproduced, stored
in a retrieval system or transmitted, in any form or by any means without the prior consent of the author, nor be otherwise circulated in any
form of binding or cover other than that with which it is published and
without a similar condition being imposed on the subsequent purchaser.

ISBNs:
978-1-913136-99-4 paperback
978-1-913340-00-1 ebook

'Don't ever lose your spark.'

For my father

Chapter 1

Nana Rose's house sat upon a hill, with a river at the bottom, trees down along the paddock and a rugged stony road leading to the door. It was miles from anywhere and, in the summer, the front door was permanently open welcoming any number of visitors, cats, birds and wildlife into the hall. The herb garden, pungent with dill and sage was overgrown and as wild as the meadows above the house. The Peters family travelled every year to see Nana but it was Emily who always insisted on staying the whole summer long whilst everyone else wanted to jet off to somewhere hot or exotic sounding. For Emily, seeing the paddock from the main road, was just the first hint of adventures to come and she was brimming with excitement for what lay ahead.

It was the first day of the summer holidays. As always, ten year old Emily had her rucksack packed the night before. She had her hair brush sticking out of the top of the ruck sack so that it was handy to brush her long brown hair whenever she wanted to. Her full water bottle was neatly tucked into the side pocket ready for the journey ahead. Emily's sister Lizzie however, who was five years older, was sitting on the floor in her bedroom with what appeared to be her entire wardrobe piled high around her wondering what to pack.

'Do you need a hand?' Emily asked standing at the door.

'I think I do,' Lizzie sighed.

Emily started to extract various items of clothing from the ring around Lizzie. 'It's a French exchange you are going on in Paris Lizzie so I'm thinking where will you be going and what will you be doing?' She held up a dress, 'Louvre,' a pair of jeans, 'Eiffel Tower,' a pale blue skirt, 'evening restaurant.' This process continued amidst lots of giggling and in no time at all, Lizzie's suitcase was full, zipped and secured with a shiny pink padlock attached. Both girls headed downstairs with their luggage to the front door where their Dad was already packing up the car.

As the car headed off down the road, Lizzie sat in the back seat and texted Lucille in Paris. Lucille was to be her French host in Paris, and the two had been pen-friends for over a year now. 'I am on my way. I'm so excited. See you soon.' Helped along with a snooze, the journey to Nana's house seemed to go quickly despite the detour to the airport to drop off Lizzie.

'Babu, Babu!' Emily shouted with glee out through the window as she saw Nana's beautiful white cat strolling stealthily down towards them as if he knew they were coming and was welcoming them.

'I hope Nana's got the kettle on,' Emily's mother, Mary, murmured to herself somewhat relieved to have reached the house before nightfall.

'If I know Mum, she'll have more than just the kettle on for us,' said Bruce, Emily's father.

As the car drew up, Emily rushed out and ran very fast around the side of the house hearing classical piano music which was loudly playing from within. She knew exactly where her Nana would be and dashed towards the kitchen shouting, 'Nana, we're here,' before rushing into her arms, all buttered hands, as her Nana Rose was putting the final touches to her yummy apple flan. A huge hug ensued that lasted until Mary arrived into the kitchen carrying gifts from the car.

The kitchen was by far the busiest room in Nana Rose's home. It was a big wide room, with washing always drying on the high rack above the racing green Aga. This was definitely the cosiest spot to sit in front of during the winter months. There was an old wooden chair that was placed at the far end of the kitchen table and, as always, Babu was already curled up on it claiming the space as his own. He was quite unfazed by the loud conversation, and clatter from the noisy visiting family.

'So, where are you going to this year?' Nana asked Mary.

'It's Greece this year. A small island called Milos. It's quite a trek I know but we are leaving the car in Manchester and flying on from there.'

Bruce gave his daughter a gentle squeeze, and whispered into Emily's ear, 'There is still time for you to come with us Emily, if you'd like?'

Emily looked up smiling with her warm big blue eyes and said, 'Dad, you know I don't like the heat and I love it here. You and Mum are to go on holiday and have a nice romantic time together on your own. Nana said last year that she would show me how to play the cello this summer.'

Bruce glanced over at Nana catching her eye, and they both looked up at the shelf beside the sideboard.

On the shelf, between the cookery books, was a large photograph frame. Emily was the only one to notice their brief glance across to the picture before Nana busily returned to her cooking. Emily strained her neck upward in the seat to look at the large photograph but before she could wriggle out from her father's arms, dinner was being served and she soon forgot about taking a closer look.

That night saw the family tucking into the tasty hot stew. The room was filled with chatter and joke telling followed by bed time and lights out. There is something about being in the countryside that just makes for a good night's slumber; especially that first night which ignited vivid dreams full of wonder for all the Peters family. Not a sound could be heard outside except for the distant call of the barn owl which sounded almost in perfect time with the grandfather clock downstairs in the hall.

The next day, Emily's parents headed off early on their travels following breakfast and Emily sat on the front step watching the car trundle down the stony paddock road, before disappearing only to rise again on the winding road going back up towards Carlisle. A tiny Dad's hand could be seen waving from the car window and Emily jumped up waving back so she could be seen.

The sun was out and fluffy white clouds moved in slow motion across the sky. The house was surrounded by a mature, somewhat rugged garden. At the top of the garden, towards the back of the house, stood an old oak tree, under which Emily liked to read in the afternoon. Emily walked along the dry-stone wall, which she thought was getting very over-grown. This year, the apples on the trees were small but plentiful.

'By the looks of things, we are going to have a bumper harvest this year Emily,' Nana said coming out into the garden to join her. 'I still have some jars of apple chutney from last year to be given away to some of my friends when they come to the house. Please remind me to take the jars from the larder when someone comes round.'

'Yes, will do,' Emily replied, always happy to help out.

'Gardener Bill is coming round this week to fix the lawn-mower, it's making a clunking noise. Can you give me a hand to do some cutting back in the herb garden?' Nana Rose turned and reached up for an apple and examined it closely for a moment pushing up her glasses as she did so. She looked funny when she squinted never sure whether she could see things better up close or at a distance.

'You'll find some secateurs on the shelf at the back of the barn.'

Emily wandered over to the barn.

'I have a hoe and a basket for the weeding,' her Nana shouted out in her soft lyrical voice.

The earthy dank air in the barn, with old rusty bikes and

bags of soil and soot in the corner, housed all sorts of equipment. *Those bikes must have been Dad's,* Emily thought, slowly shaking her head trying to imagine anyone being able to even attempt to cycle up all the high fells close to the house. Dad liked his sailing though and it was a pity to see his old Dart 18 dinghy sitting unused on a trailer with the tyres long deflated at the far end of the barn.

After a short spell of work in the garden, Emily ventured off towards the oak tree behind the house to see the two horses, Molly and Milly, she had not seen since last year. She fed them with lots of long grass from Nana's garden, seeing as the horses had munched their own grass down to the very tiniest of shoots. It felt so good to be back and to savour the long afternoon outside in the meadow accompanied by Babu who was happy to tag along. Emily sat down at the foot of the old oak tree, which was a peaceful place to read. She loved the sound of the birds that nested high in the branches. Babu, who had been curled up asleep beside her, yawned and stretched before getting to his feet at dusk. Emily closed her book and followed the cat back through the orchard.

Chapter 2

The next morning, it was a bit chilly inside the house. Emily looked out of her bedroom window and noticed that it had been raining overnight. Nana had spent the morning upstairs in her study and Emily could hear the soft classical music playing from her room.

Nana taught piano lessons and her pupils came from far and wide in the local community for their weekly tuition. Nana Rose had decided to cut back on having so many pupils to just teaching two days a week so that she could spend more time reading in her study and working on her research and studies. Emily was never quite sure what these studies were but Nana had obtained a number of degrees at university in her younger days. She was always working on some project or other with her love of English and History.

Heading downstairs and to the kitchen, Babu was sitting on his chair sleeping and Emily decided to make herself some toast from the freshly baked bread cooling on the rack. 'Oh Babu,' she sighed, 'What are we going to do this afternoon?' The cat's tail moved from side to side lightly on the cushion. 'I thought I could do some drawing and maybe draw you, if you stay seated in that chair of yours,' she smiled. Whilst carving the bread, Emily's eye caught the reflection of the photograph on the shelf, which she had seen her Nana glancing at the night she had arrived.

Taking a bite of toast, Emily reached up to bring the frame closer. In the picture was a man standing with a cello. It must have been a very old photo because it was black and white and had gone slightly yellowish around the edges. The man was young, tall and very handsome. She did not recognise, nor had she seen this man in any of the other photographs around the house. Puzzled, she slumped down at the kitchen table with Babu loudly purring from his chair. 'A cello,' Emily said out loud to herself. 'Where is the cello? I'm sure Nana promised me she would teach me an instrument and I'm sure she said a cello.' Emily went to the music room with this thought in her mind.

The room was blue and white in colour with white porcelain vases and what Nana had said was William Morris wallpaper. There were two huge sash windows which flooded the room in daylight, ideal for her Nana's practice each day and piano lessons. She looked around and, apart from the baby grand piano, there were no other instruments in there. Curious, but not wanting to disturb her Nana's studies, she pondered whether she had seen a cello or case anywhere else in the house. As she stood there, Babu walked past the door and she followed him into the hall and up the staircase to the landing. He led her further up yet more stairs which she had not really noticed before at the back of the house and she walked quietly along the carpeted creaky floor.

At the end of the landing, a small white handle was teased open gently and with one tiny jolt, the narrow door opened revealing a steep staircase which led up to what appeared to be the attic. Babu and Emily climbed the staircase on all fours. A small roof window meant that there was no need to switch on the light and heavy raindrops could be heard clattering against the glass. The door closed behind them startling them both and Babu sped across the attic floor and meowed. 'Shhh,' she said, knowing her Nana would not mind her exploring the house; but somehow creeping about a room she had never been in or knew about felt a bit strange. Babu hopped up on an old wooden chest of drawers and curled his tail about his paws. Across from the cat, two large black cases lay on the floor. Both cases, although similar in shape, differed in size. Other than the two cases, the room was empty except for an old wobbly kitchen chair and some old velvet curtains Nana had removed some time back when decorating the sitting room.

Eager to find out what was inside the cases, Emily placed her hand across the larger of the two.

'L.T.P.' she read out under her breath as her hand brushed over the three initials embossed on the top of the dusty case. She opened the latches and to her absolute delight she discovered the most beautiful instrument she had ever seen. The reddish-brown full-size cello had an ornately carved scroll with its four black oval tuning pegs. She touched each of the strings one at a time, with the big one first through to the thinnest one. They were loose so she could not pluck them or hear them make a sound. Not wanting to lift the cello out because it looked so delicate, she rifled through the velvet pockets inside. She found a small glass bottle with an oily yellowish liquid inside, and what looked like a box with something like the amber which her father collected. Her father's amber contained fossils inside but this piece did not. She didn't know anything about string instruments but knew there were always lots of parts and bits of things needed to keep the instruments in good working order.

Emily looked up quizzically at Babu and listened to his loud purring that was now seemingly even louder than the raindrops above them. Emily stood up to stroke him and, as he stretched out in appreciation, he knocked over a small pewter pot that stood upon the drawers. The pot fell down and rolled under the chest of drawers, so Emily knelt down, placing her cheek on the floor and stretched out her hand to retrieve it. As she did so, she noticed that something rectangular was wedged behind the chest.

Sliding the heavy chest away from the wall with all her strength, she pulled out an old dusty leather satchel. 'L.T.P.' she read out loud. *These were the same initials embossed on the case*, she thought. Emily hesitated to open the satchel, which was not hers to touch. Her hands moved over the catch and it clicked open unexpectedly. Emily hesitantly opened the satchel. Inside was a rather tall book. It was a slender, dark green paper book and when she pulled it out, she realised that it was actually a music manuscript book. Each page was filled with handwritten notes. Notes meaning music notes. She didn't know then, but they were written as music notation for cello and piano. Beautifully scripted and not one error in the black scrawling ink, she flicked slowly through the pages. Apart from the music notes, there did not appear to be any words or titles or even a signature to provide some clue as to who wrote the music.

Conscious that she had been up in the room some time, and a little bewildered about the cellos and the music notebook, with many questions flying through her mind to ask Nana, she returned the bottle and amber back into the pocket. She picked up the leather satchel, placed the music notebook back inside and pushed the satchel under the chest of drawers. She knelt down beside the chair, closed up the cello case and clambered back down the steep stairs and onto the landing. Emily carefully closed the door after Babu was safely down. Nana was in the kitchen preparing food and whistling to herself. On the table were drawing pencils and paper ready for Emily to draw fashion costumes which her Nana knew she liked to do as a pastime.

'Nana, who is the man in the photo up there?' Emily asked, pointing up to the shelf.

Nana brought the potatoes over to the table to be peeled, and sat down. Drawing in a breath, she smiled warmly at Emily with her kind eyes. 'That's my brother Leni and he very sadly left home when I was about three or so years older than you. He was my older brother; I only had the one and that's the last photo that was taken in this house shortly before he left.'

Emily listened intently wide eyed and wanting to learn about everything. 'Why did he leave the house and where did he go; why didn't you hear from him?'

'Well Emily, you see, it was a mystery for me really. He was very bright, an intellectual, and during World War II he would have enlisted as a soldier and been posted overseas. He was a marvellous mimic who was also bilingual. In the photograph you can see that he was a young man and would have joined the military. We believe he would have spent the war in France due to his linguistic ability, but the circumstances of what happened during the war and his involvement is not something that we were able to find out about as a family.'

'Where in France?' Emily asked.

'Well, we presumed Paris maybe because this was the capital and this city was under occupation by the Germans in the war. Due to his ability to be able to speak with differing French accents, meant that he could take on a southern French accent or a part of Paris for example that most people couldn't imitate, and hide his English accent too; he would have blended in as if a Parisian quite easily. Having said that, he could have blended into any number of French cities or towns across France. We simply don't know. I was very young but I remember my parents explaining that we could get little information about where Leni had gone, and everything seemed to be very secretive. Perhaps he was a spy. I have read books about the war and many spies were chosen due to their linguistic ability which would have been helpful to the British Forces.'

Emily was transfixed by the story of her Great Uncle Leni and tried to imagine where he would have been and what role he would have played potentially as a British spy. She also wondered why he would not have contacted the family.

'Surely, he wrote to you during the war to tell you how he was?' Emily asked.

10

'That is a very astute question, but we did not receive any letters. My parents would have told me if they had. They did not. Again, maybe this was due to Leni having had a special responsibility, or the secrecy of his mission, but I have read about it and again never found there to be any real leads to help me find out what had happened to my brother.' Emily tried her best to think of a way to research his whereabouts in the hope of tracing him. Her Nana could see her worried facial expression and tried to reassure her.

'Emily,' she said, 'For years I have tried to find the answers. I went to Paris myself a few times during my late twenties, meeting with officials, but there was so much confidentiality surrounding those times and getting records and not knowing where to start was very difficult. My parents did receive a letter from the military stating 'Ultimate Fate Unknown' after the Second World War, which I later knew to mean that he was missing in action and presumed dead. I, of course, did not really settle with this as an answer and that is why I went to Paris myself.' Nana put the frame back onto the shelf and said, 'After all these years I still do miss him terribly. Now, how about a warm cup of cocoa?'

Emily estimated that he must have been about twenty years old in the photo.

'He's standing with a cello. Nana, you mentioned last year that you could teach me how to play the instrument?'

Emily hoped her Nana would tell her about the cellos up in the attic, but instead Nana dismissed her words and said, 'I remember from last year, and yes, I would love to show you the cello and play the cello with you but I have not played ever since my brother left and I don't know why I happened to say to you that I would teach you but I am not really sure that I can.'

Babu resumed his seat near to the Aga and her Nana stroked the cat next to her, sitting deep in thought as the potatoes simmered on the stove.

The next day, the sun shone brightly and Nana was up early ready for her first piano pupil of the day. Emily enjoyed chatting to the families as they waited in the kitchen during the lessons whilst hearing the faint sounds of voices and piano playing in the nearby music room. Sometimes the visitors to the house were old friends Nana had taught for many years and sometimes children her own age came along and waited their turn in her company.

Emily was keen to walk up to see the horses with her friend Charlotte when she visited the house. Charlotte had been taking piano lessons for the past three years and Emily and Charlotte had become good friends. On their way back from seeing the horses, Bill the gardener, could be heard driving up the hill in his old red truck.

'Hi Bill, how are you?' Emily called out.

'Hi there Emily, you are visiting your Nana again this year! You are getting very tall now!'

'Yes, I'm staying for the summer, and this is Charlotte. We've just fed the horses, and made these daisy chains.' Both girls twirled round to show their daisy crowns, whilst Bill smiled a toothless grin.

'Shall I let Nana know you are here?'

The elderly man shook his head. 'No need. Your Nana has already given me a list of tasks as long as my arm.'

Emily and Charlotte peered into the back of Bill's truck which was full of tools. They stood back whilst Bill lifted out a long, dangerous looking hedge trimmer.

'Emily, I'm going back in, I think my music lesson must be about to start,' Charlotte whispered. Charlotte skipped into the house and Emily stayed outside with Bill.

'Nana said that the lawnmower is broken, and it needs fixing.' Emily said.

'Oh yes, I'll get to that tomorrow Emily. Today I'm going to sort out the hedge that runs down to the paddock. I do know that your Nana has wanted this cut back for some time,' Bill paused and rubbed his back, 'But this is a big old farm and I tackle it one job at a time.' Emily brought out some tea and biscuits and left old Bill to it.

Emily had the run of the house, seeing as her Nana was teaching. Her mind kept racing back to the cellos and what Nana had said the night before. She took a walk down to the river, with Babu at her side, and threw some small sticks in to watch them float by in the dark water.

'I wonder if Nana would show me how to play the cello?' Emily spoke out loud to the cat, as if he would look up at her and answer her questions at any moment. 'What happened to Great Uncle Leni, and what did he do in the Second World War if he had been a spy? Where would he have worked?' Fascinated by the fact that he had spoken French fluently, as well as the mystery surrounding his disappearance, Emily wished she could learn more about her Great Uncle Leni. He looked so smart and proud with his cello, she thought. She looked directly at the cat to see him chasing a small spider in the grass. *It is such a shame the cellos have been locked away in their cases for so long. They should be played*, she thought.

Although Emily had not opened the second case, she knew that cellos came in a variety of sizes and if Leni had had a full-size cello then he must have started with a smaller cello and maybe that was what was in the other case. *The perfect size for me to start with*, she thought.

Nana continued teaching her piano lessons the following day, but instead of Emily welcoming visitors into the kitchen and chatting, she went back up to the attic and opened the second case. As suspected, there was another cello in the case. She closed her eyes and drew in a long deep breath through her nose taking in the dense richness of the old wood. *What a lovely smell*, she thought. Emily knew she had to tell her Nana that she had found the room and the cellos and that she so wanted to hear what they sounded like.

Nana had prepared a lovely log fire that evening, and after

bath time, Emily came back downstairs to sit in front of the fire so that her Nana could brush her long brown hair. Her hair would always dry nicely in front of the fire before going to bed. The flames settled to a warm orange hue.

'Nana,' Emily said and turned her head looking upwards. Emily hesitated to find the right words but her thoughts came out in a flurry. 'Babu took me to the room upstairs and I found the cellos in the attic.'

Her Nana smiled warmly, resting both her hands gently on Emily's shoulders.

'Curious cat our Babu. I'm not surprised he took you up there.' Her Nana resumed brushing her long hair with slow, long strokes. 'I've been thinking a lot about my brother recently. He started learning the cello around about your age and when he developed his playing, he showed me how to play. I was never as good as him, of course, but he had a gift for playing the cello. He picked up that instrument and made it sing! He was a great composer too, always making up his own tunes and I would play them on the piano with him when he wrote them down. We had so much fun. Always fun with my brother.' Her voice trailed off and Emily looked ahead into the fire, tuning into the crackling sound that was making her feel sleepy.

'Nana, I think we should bring the cellos down to this room and dust them down and I think you should show me how to play. It seems such a pity them being up there and I'm sure you would enjoy hearing them again.'

Taken with Emily's longing to learn the cello, her Nana remembered her brother's inquisitive mind and self motivation that he applied to everything he did. When he got to thinking about something, he wanted to follow his heart and there was no stopping him, she thought. Her Nana loved to see this quality in Emily and knew it was only right that these cellos come out of that dusty attic room and be brought down and be given their place in the music room again. She too had long wanted to hear them, if truth be told; their resonance and deep tone created such a wonderful evocative sound.

Leni's cello sang to her in her dreams of late, the low register and the music coming back to her with her brother playing so beautifully. Maybe if she played the cello again her brother would come back to her more in her dreams, she thought wistfully. This was her last thought as her head rested into her rich goose down pillow that night.

Chapter 3

Emily awoke early and dashed downstairs to help herself to a bowl of cereal. A fresh, cool breeze was blowing through the house. Emily took her bowl and sat down on the front step and munched at her breakfast.

'Morning Emily,' Nana called from the end of the garden, where she was already busy picking wild raspberries and blackberries ready for a fruit crumble later in the day.

The sunny, clear day, soaked up the early morning dew and Emily fed the cats, leaving a bowl outside for the country feral cats that never came inside the house but loved getting fed, nevertheless.

When Nana came back into the kitchen, she set a bowl brimming with fruit on the table. She went over to the Belfast sink and washed and dried her hands before turning to Emily.

'Emily, follow me.'

Nana opened the door to the music room and ushered Emily in. Next to the piano were two chairs, a music stand and two beautiful cellos lying on their side on the carpet with their bows placed on top.

Emily shrieked with excitement and jumped with joy. She hugged her Nana and rushed over to the cellos.

Nana pulled out some of the old cello books from the shelf she had used when she was a little girl. Opening the first one, Emily saw the lovely handwriting with the name 'Leni' written in the top right-hand side of the page. The books were very old but so beautifully preserved.

'Can we play them now, Nana?'

'Soon, my dear, first we need to get them back into good working order.'

Getting dusting cloths from the kitchen, Nana and Emily proceeded to take great care and dust each of the instruments. Emily touched the curved smooth edge of the cello lightly. There was a little mould on the spike of the cellos so the spikes needed to be taken out and properly cleaned. The strings were very old and the cellos needed new sets which had to be bought to replace them. Charlotte's father, who owned the music shop, had agreed to drop round two new sets of strings the following day. Once replaced, the cellos were ready to be tuned by Nana.

Emily took up her seat opposite Nana Rose, and plucked each string in turn.

'This is an A, this is D, this is G and the big string is a C,' she said.

They plucked each string together and Emily said the string names out loud to herself.

'Nana, will you play me a tune?'

Nana thought for a moment, closed her eyes, picked up her bow that had been rosined and dusted down and played a short melody.

It was as if she was going back in time all those years ago playing alongside her brother sitting opposite her. The sound was vivid and clear, and when she played, the memory of her brother was so real to her as if she pictured him playing wearing his navy blue jumper, making jokes and grinning at her. It was such a pleasure to be playing the cellos again.

Chapter 4

The train drew into Gare du Nord at precisely 2:15 in the afternoon on the 4th May 1943. The shining green doors swung open with an outpouring of soldiers, army officers, civilians and children hurriedly crisscrossing with their suitcases off the train and onto the platform edge. The sound of clattering high heels and loud footsteps peppered the air as a floodgate of passengers walked out from the murky gloom towards the 'sortie', meaning 'exit' in French.

Henri Berger was one of the last few passengers to step out onto the platform. He placed his suitcase down and stood up straight, positioning his hat with a crisp newspaper held under his arm. He was striking, tall and dashingly handsome. His dark brown hair was now hidden from view and he wore a bespoke tailored suit. He walked relaxed and dapper, his stride long and languid. He continued walking past two train attendants who were shortly to finish their shift. 'Pardon,' a woman with bright red lipstick and blushed cheeks apologised as she accidentally knocked into him on her way to platform three. Her accent was from southern Paris, he thought to himself.

'Ausweis,' a German officer demanded. This sinister figure stood at a pillar with a blank expression on his face, asking passengers for their relevant papers which everyone had to carry with them in Paris at that time as they moved about the occupied city.

The day was grey with the threat of rain. A sea of coats and scarves moved in the grand square at the station's main gates. Henri stepped into a waiting car and was driven to his apartment. For nearly a year, he walked between his small apartment and his office. Twice a day he made the route across the Jardin des Tuileries; always deliberate in his stride and giving little consideration to the small crocuses blooming at the side of the walk ways.

Henri was awaiting a specific day that eventually arrived. He knew that his apartment was most probably being bugged with listening devices and never at any moment did he let down his guard. Even singing in the shower, his favourite past time back home, had to be eradicated in order that not a hint of his true origin could be given away. Every movement and every trait were considered and acted out. He was the authentic Frenchman and not even a local batted an eye.

'Bonjour Monsieur Berger.' An elderly lady who mopped the stairs every morning, spoke quietly in the echoey corridor. Henri nodded politely, tipped his hat towards her and smiled charismatically. He strolled lightly past her to the foot of the stairs, his fragrance dense and rich which hung in the air for some time after he had passed her by.

Henri walked his usual route across the park but unlike any other day, he stopped four benches away from the East Gate and sat down. It was now one o'clock. He had not looked at his watch since 12:45 but knew the exact time to the last second. He brought a jam sandwich out from his left pocket and unwrapped it. He was to wait four minutes and leave if a woman with a pram did not pass him. At precisely 13:03, a tall and elegant lady wearing a grey woollen jacket walked in front of him, pushing a large pram before her. She took a seat at the other end of the bench. She picked up her baby from the pram and cradled her on her lap. The woman lay a tiny brown envelope down to her right-hand side and Henri reached out to touch the baby's arm, leaning over to look directly into the baby's big blue eyes as she bounced gleefully on her mother's knee. Her tiny white ribbons fluttered in the breeze.

With sleight of hand, Henri lifted the envelope and wrapped it into his napkin with the remains of his half-eaten sandwich. Looking up at the sky, he signaled rain as a gesture to the stranger by his side before standing, smoothing down his jacket and continuing his regular path to the office.

As the storm took hold, Henri's dark figure darted across the puddles and he raised his lapels higher to shelter himself against the stiff breeze that had whipped up. A little tune fleetingly crossed his mind and he hummed it to himself in the rain. After reaching the offices, he spent the afternoon working. Later in the day, Henri had to meet someone north of the city, so he decided to walk on foot through the streets passing shops and vendors, blending in with the local people with his flawless ability to speak the native language whenever he had to talk to others.

Shutters began to close ready for the night's curfew and people began to desert the streets, heading inside their homes and dwellings. The apartment blocks were tall and dark. He picked up his walking pace and went down the dark steps into the depths of the Metro at Porte de la Chapelle.

There was no warning. The deafening loud crack from above was split second in timing. The hit was direct. The allied bombings devastated the Metro station and the surrounding area. There was little time for people to escape and run away to safety. Many people lost their lives that day in the Paris underground. Fires broke out and buildings such as warehouses, offices and apartment blocks burned to the ground. It was to be the worst bombing in Paris during the Second World War.

Chapter 5

The hospital room was white. Henri opened his eyes for the first time since the blast. He could hardly move and when he tried, he felt a terrible pain in his chest.

A kind nurse had seen that he had awoken and gently placed a reassuring hand on his shoulder before calling the doctor. 'It's okay, you are in hospital and you will be fine.' A tired looking doctor entered the room with a clip-board tucked under his arm. The doctor walked over to the patient's bed.

'I am pleased to see you awake,' the doctor said. 'You are a very lucky man.' The doctor took out a small torch and peered into each of Henri's eyes. 'Can you tell us your name?' the doctor asked, putting the torch back into the top pocket of his white coat.

Henri's head was aching and so too were his chest and legs. Henri opened his mouth but realised that he did not actually know what his name was. He closed his eyes to think but nothing came. 'I don't know,' he said frustrated. 'I really don't know who I am.'

'Do you remember what happened to you?'

Henri thought again and shook his head. 'I don't remember anything, what is wrong with me?'

'You were caught in a bomb blast and took a serious blow to your head,' the doctor explained. 'It is important you get some rest and we will talk again when you have slept a little more.'

Henri's recovery was slow and he lay quietly most of the day to begin the healing process whilst trying to recall who he was and what had happened to him. More than two weeks passed by and Henri began to sit up and speak to the other patients in the ward listening to their stories. A young man told him that Porte de la Chapelle had been severely bombed and that there had been many people killed. He himself had had a very bad injury to his left arm and leg and had to have both limbs bound up in bandages.

Although his headaches had subsided, Henri could not remember what had happened to him and the hospital staff explained that he had suffered loss of memory and that they were unable to find any form of identification to find out who he was. Once he had fully recovered from his injuries and was allowed to leave the care of the hospital, he was provided with new identification papers with the new name Bertrand Poitier.

Chapter 6

During the days that Nana was busy teaching, Emily did not practise her cello but instead chose to read, chat to the many visitors to the house or lay in the garden. Bill, the gardener, managed to fix the lawnmower and Emily kept him company, helping out with the weeding in the herb garden and collecting some of the hedge trimmings into a wheelbarrow before wheeling them over to the compost heap at the back of the garden. She made them both tea and baked some current slices which she shared with everyone at the house. Emily wore her Nana's apron, which went down below her knees, gardening gloves and wellies most of the time and picked flowers for her Nana's vase on the kitchen table. She replaced them every day or every other day depending on whether they had wilted. There were two house martin nests in the eaves and Emily could see the little chicks popping their heads out from time to time chirping when they were being brought food.

When Nana was not teaching piano lessons, Emily returned to her cello practice. Nana said that her progress in learning the cello was very good, and after the first week Nana had shown her how to place the bow on the strings, using just 'a half bow,' which meant that instead of her hand being at the heel of the bow, it rested half way along. This technique helped Emily get used to using the bow on the strings and developed the stamina required to practise the 'up' and 'down' bowing correctly.

Nana shared her love of music recordings and introduced Emily to many different cello and classical music composers. Emily listened to all the great works, such as the Shostakovich Cello Concerto No. 1 in E-flat major, the Bach Cello Suites and Beethoven Cello Sonatas. They listened to the recorded orchestral and chamber music through the open music room windows, during the afternoon when they were both outside in the garden. Nana Rose enjoyed sharing stories of her childhood, growing up in a happy home with her parents and life with her brother Leni before the war.

Nana taught Emily to play the C and G major scales and played them through on the piano to assist with her intonation so she would learn to play them in tune. The routine and structure for Emily's cello lessons were to start with learning the scales, followed by some technique exercises and then working through two or three melodies that she had picked out from a selection that her Nana had played to her previously. Emily would often take the cello up to her room to continue her practice between the lesson times.

Emily dreamt of cellos when she slept and started to draw them at the kitchen table instead of always drawing costumes and dresses. She would close her eyes and think of the beautiful melodies, of concert halls and duet performances, of the life of a cellist touring the world.

One day when she was laying on her bed, daydreaming wistfully, Nana Rose could be heard playing the baby grand piano downstairs in the music room. Emily noticed that she was only playing the right-hand melody. She listened intently waiting for the left-hand bass part to be added with the right hand but the music would stop in the same place each time and was only played with one hand. Emily listened for some time before her Nana stopped playing and then she ran downstairs to find her Nana getting up from the piano stool and closing the lid. 'Nana, why did you not play the music fully with both hands?' Emily asked. Her Nana led her out into the kitchen and settled at the kitchen table with Babu at her side.

'I remember your Great Uncle Leni playing the repeated melody that I was just playing. It was his own music composition. He used to play it on the cello, and I would accompany him on the piano. I would tell him that I thought it would be a major hit in the classical music world and that he should publish it,' she chuckled. 'It's very distinctive don't you think?'

'Yes it is. Nana, where is the music for it?'

'I don't know,' her Nana responded, 'I looked on the shelves and couldn't find it. It must have disappeared, it was such a long time ago,' she said. Nana Rose stroked Babu and kissed his nose.

Emily jumped up and said, 'Nana, would you like a cup of tea?' Slightly taken aback with Emily's haste and sudden rushing about, her Nana said, 'Oh yes dear, that would be very nice, thank you.'

Emily opened the Aga plate lid, filled the kettle and made her Nana a pot of tea. She chopped a thin slice of plum cake and placed the teapot, teacup and cake on a tray and brought it to the table for her Nana to savour. Leaving her Nana to enjoy her afternoon tea, Emily disappeared upstairs to the attic where the cellos had been stored for so many years. She could not contain her excitement as she entered and grabbed the leather satchel, she had discovered that first day she had ventured into the room.

Emily took the satchel to her bedroom, dusted it down with a towel and took out the music notebook inside. *This must be the music that Nana was playing,* she thought to herself.

Emily returned to the kitchen where her Nana was busy washing up.

'Nana, can you come into the sitting room?' Emily called

from the door. As her Nana walked into the room, she saw the leather satchel on the coffee table. She recognised it immediately. Sitting down on the sofa, she reached forward and gently touched each of the initials on the case. She opened the satchel and pulled out the manuscript notebook from inside. Delicately and slowly she opened the notebook and read the first few bars of the piano and cello composition. Tears silently streamed down her face and she brushed them away and smiled lovingly at her granddaughter who was sitting, eyes wide open and sparkling bright.

'Is this the music Nana? The satchel was behind the chest of drawers in the attic.'

'Yes, it is,' Nana replied. 'Let's go and play it.'

They both went into the music room and Nana played the unfinished composition without a note out of place on the piano. Throughout the summer months, Emily hummed and whistled the tune in the bath, shower and outside in the garden. When she took her skipping rope outside, she skipped in time to the melody. There were a number of music pieces in the little notebook, but this was by far her favourite and, as it turned out, the favourite of her Nana Rose.

Emily continued to lug the cello up and down the stairs throughout her summer holiday practising, sometimes twice daily, but only for short periods in order to rest her fingers which were a little sore until she got used to pressing the strings down on the fingerboard. What she enjoyed most was learning little hornpipes with her Nana playing as a duet with her. On the telephone to her mother, Emily spoke of her daily progress and her parents agreed that she could have cello lessons following the summer and would look at the adverts for teachers in the local music shop in Norwich as soon as they arrived home.

On the last day, before the long drive back, Emily awoke to her Nana playing the piano downstairs and to the happy little tune discovered in the notebook. She lay on her bed with her eyes open, looking out to the oak tree from under the open gap in the sash window. The centuries old branches swayed in the gentle breeze as if moving to the soft lilting sounds of the piano.

At midday the family arrived, entering noisily into the house with Emily greeting everyone with a warm hug. The whole family were tired from the long drive and Lizzie sat straight down to drink the freshly prepared lemonade in the kitchen.

'So how did you get on?' Emily asked her big sister.

'It was amazing, Lucille was great fun and we went all over the place visiting every gallery and museum. We walked our feet off. We went to the Louvre, the Pompidou Centre, Montmartre and the Eiffel Tower and we had lots of picnics so we didn't have to spend too much money on eating out. It was good because Lucille's parents are really laidback so they just let us travel on our own and her mum prepared lunches for us so we could sit in the lovely parks there.'

'I hope you were safe and stuck together at all times,' Lizzie's mum asked in a slightly worried tone.

'Yes, we got on really well and it was great because Lucille travels quite a lot on public transport so I was able to use my French skills to buy tickets and find out where we needed to go by asking for directions, so I really think I improved my French and by the end of it I was speaking quite fluently. I think I understand more than I can actually speak though.' Lizzie was very mature for her age and looked much older in age than she actually was so people tended to treat her more like an adult.

'Where did you stay and what was it like?' Nana Rose asked as she prepared lunch for the family. 'The French have such great style. I love their clothes and love of art and their aesthetics,' she said.

'We stayed in their house which is north of Paris on the outskirts. It's really easy to get into the centre but it was nice to be away from the busy streets. We spent some time at Lucille's grandfather's house which wasn't far from their own home. In fact, we cycled around the parks and visited his house a few times. Lucille is very close to her grandfather and often her mum would cook a meal and she would carry it round to his home on the front of her bike so we spent a lot of time cycling over there. The whole family are lovely people, you would really like them Nana.'

'I'm sure I would!' Nana replied, serving the Caesar salad and settling down to eat lunch. 'So when is Lucille coming to stay with you all?' Nana asked. 'October holidays for just over a fortnight,' Lizzie answered.

Lizzie's mum asked politely, 'Nana Rose, we were thinking of spending the first week taking Lucille to the North Norfolk Coast for walks along the beach and to show her Norwich and take her to the castle, the cathedral and museums but thought that the second week, we could come and bring her up here. Would that be ok?'

'I'd be delighted,' Nana said. 'Does she like horse riding? Maybe we can organise a couple of mornings taking the girls out riding on a trek?'

'That would be so cool,' Lizzie and Emily answered in unison delighted at the idea.

'I'm sure she would love it!' Lizzie replied. 'She plays the flute too so I'll ask her to bring it along and I'm sure she would enjoy the fresh Cumbrian countryside air.'

'We can take her on one of the motorboats for the day on the Norfolk Broads too,' Emily's father added. Bruce loved being on the water, no matter what type of boat, whether a sailboat or motorboat. He knew the Broads like the back of his hand and often sailed with his friend Tom. 'Do you think Lucille would be interested in learning about the waterways? Maybe we could find a good spot for drawing and take along a picnic perhaps if the weather is nice?' Bruce nudged playfully into Emily who was busy serving lasagna and seemingly lost in thought.

'An adventure holiday the first week and relaxing in the Cumbrian country house the second week sounds like a good plan,' she nodded. The family continued to chatter tucking heartily into their meal following the long drive. During dessert, Emily announced, 'Well I have a surprise for you all. After you have eaten your lunch, I'll show you!'

Excitedly the family gathered in the music room. Emily and her Nana sat down to play the cellos and performed a short duet together.

'I have been learning the whole summer and I know a few tunes now!' she declared.

Her parents marvelled at the beautiful sound Nana and Emily made together.

'It's so lovely to see the cellos being played again,' Emily's Dad reflected, knowing there were cellos in the house some-where that belonged to Uncle Leni whose disappearance was never discussed during his own upbringing due to the heartbreak felt within the family.

After playing two pieces, they ended their performance and as they were putting the cellos away, Nana Rose announced to everyone, 'Emily, I am so pleased that you are learning this precious instrument. I know you don't have a cello of your own, so I would like to give you this one to take home to practise and to keep up the good work of learning each day.' Emily could not believe it and hugged her Nana tightly. 'Look after it and bring it back with you when you visit so we can play together again soon.' Emily was beyond excited and swore to herself that she would dust it and safely store it in the case and take good care of it. She knew she would practise every day and looked forward to being able to play cello pieces with her Nana accompanying her on the piano.

As the family departed, the cello case had to be laid across the knees of both Lizzie and Emily all the way home on the journey. Not wanting to ask to borrow the music notebook from the house, Emily had taken photos, using her iPad, of her favourite melody and hoped that she would be able to play the music herself to show her Nana next time she visited. The family drove away and Emily turned to wave out of the back window. She saw Babu, who had wandered down to the paddock to see them off.

Chapter 7

It was not until the October holidays that Lucille arrived to spend what was just over a fortnight for her French exchange at the Peters' home in Norfolk. Picking her up from the airport Emily was under strict instructions to talk only in English so that Lucille could practise the language. Happily, she was quite fluent already and Emily was the first to run into the house showing her each room to make her feel welcome and at home.

The fifteen-year-old friends were already close, and they soon hung out together in Lizzie's bedroom listening to music and watching TV. Their mum had prepared a detailed itinerary for their plans over the course of the trip and first up they went to the North Norfolk coastline for a long walk. Driving into Burnham Overy Staithe, the family walked along the narrow path with the tide out and saw all sorts of birds and wildlife. They had taken along their small sketchbooks and drew the landscape with the boats sunken into the mud. There was a multitude of all kinds of birds busily searching for food in the falling tide. The beautiful Norfolk Broads were a great place to see otters and kingfishers, so Emily went sailing with her Dad whilst the girls sketched from the shore.

Walking at dusk along the pebble beach near the small village of Kelling, the family were delighted to see a seal pop its head up out of the water as they were strolling along. Emily whistled the tune she loved hearing at her Nana's house and the seal bobbed up for a couple of minutes before diving down into the water for about five minutes to feed, before returning back to the surface again. Lucille was sure that it was the tune that kept the seal from swimming away, so joined in to see if the seal would stay longer with them. The seal kept returning to the surface, but it was the girls who needed to head back before it got dark, so they waved the seal goodbye.

One day they took a trip into the city and Emily headed over to The Classic Cafe with her mother whilst the other girls went shopping. She loved hearing the classical music that played as backing music in the cafe and the wide beams across the ceiling. They met up to go to the cinema that was not far away and travelled back later in the day.

Emily practiced her cello most days and one day Lucille came into the music room and asked her about the instrument.

'In France we say, 'violoncelle'. You are playing very well,' she said, clapping in appreciation.

Emily had been attending weekly lessons and loved learning with her cello teacher, Lotte. She showed her the G major scale which uses the same notes going up and going down; she learned the A minor melodic scale which has notes that go up differently to the notes going down.

'I am trying to play this tune,' Emily showed Lucille the iPad with the music she had photographed back at her Nana's home. 'It is quite difficult, but I can play the first part. I do not have the ending because the music was never finished, but I love the melody on the cello.'

'Why was the music unfinished?' Lucille enquired.

Emily explained the story of how she had discovered the cello in the attic at her Nana Rose's house; how she had found an old satchel with a music notebook inside and also explained why the music composition had not been completed. Lucille went upstairs and returned with her flute and tried playing the little tune herself. The register was higher but with the same notes, and the melody was still as catchy and memorable. Lucille was able to sight read the music quite easily. Lucille took photos of Emily with her cello and videoed them both playing the little melody so that she could show her friends and keep a record. She had to prepare a presentation of her visit so she took her camera everywhere.

The family travelled up to see Nana Rose for the second week of the French exchange. Emily's mother drove the three girls up on the long drive and they took a slight detour so that Lucille could see the beautiful variety of countryside in England as they weaved their way towards Cumbria. Emily's favourite was the Peak District with its purple heather adorning the fells and dark peat soil darkening the landscape. Lucille loved the tiny villages and the changes of the terrain. The family sang along to songs from the radio and they played 'I spy' in French and English to test their vocabulary.

Nana was part way through a piano lesson when the family arrived, so they settled in the kitchen until she was finished for the day. The autumnal months brought a change to the garden and an assortment of new fruits and colours. There was always a stiff breeze up on top of the hill at that time of the year so the front door had to remain closed and Babu preferred to be inside apart from joining Emily when she went out for her walks around the garden and up to the oak tree.

'Bienvenue,' Nana Rose beamed welcoming Lucille. Nana Rose spoke fluent French and felt an immediate connection with Lucille as she also liked cooking and Lucille loved baking. This was a time to exchange recipes and Lucille was very keen to cook on the Aga and prepare food for the family. The larder contained plenty of ingredients to work with and Lucille also took delight in looking through all the items in the well-stocked fridge to see what was available before flicking through Nana Rose's huge collection of cookery books. With the girls stroking Babu in his chair, Lucille took lots of photos and said that it would be a good idea to create a blog of her visit for her school project. Nana Rose agreed to playing the backing music on the piano for any video clips and Lucille would collate the photos from her visit. Emily was tasked with taking photos of the garden and Lizzie and Lucille would create a dialogue in French and English.

'A busy bee's work is never done,' Nana proclaimed, her favourite saying, as the girls gathered round the table to set out their plans.

Nana Rose was teaching most of the following day and Lizzie and Emily's mum went off shopping in Carlisle. It was raining and Lucille had a slight cold, so she decided to stay inside with Emily for the day hoping to get better. Sitting in the kitchen, the girls worked on the blog together.

Lucille noticed the shelf of photos and the old photo of the young man with his cello. 'Is this your Great Uncle Leni?' Lucille asked.

'Yes, it is.'

'He looks so young and is that the cello you are playing?'

'Oh no, that's the full-size one in the music room that Nana plays and the half-size one is the cello that she used to learn on when she was my age.' Emily showed Lucille the original music notebook and she carefully looked at each page taking her time to read the music as best she could.

'What is the tune you are playing?' Lucille asked and Emily whistled it out loud and pointed it out in the book.

'It is a pity the music ends, there's actually more music written for the piano part but the cello part is mostly unfinished,' Lucille said. Emily had a better understanding of how to read music notation now and could see what she meant. Lucille took a photo of the notebook and the music with its beautifully handwritten music notation.

Later that evening Emily played Nana her pieces and demonstrated how well she had progressed with her technique, exercises and scales. 'Nana,' she said, 'Can you play the piece from the book and I will play along with my cello?' Emily could play the first several bars of the distinctive melody and upon hearing this, Lucille came into the room.

'Encore,' she said and filmed the duet for her blog. Her Nana was very impressed with Emily's progress. Emily said that her music teacher also had a cat and that she had the most amazing plants in the window of her music room. When they were watered, they smelled of lemons.

'That must be lemon verbena plants. They grow tall and give out the most amazing aroma,' Nana said, 'my mother always had those plants in this house when we were children.'

'That's interesting. My grandfather loves the smell and has those plants in his house too,' said Lucille.

The family more or less stayed in the house over the next few days due to the heavy rain that poured down most of the day. It did not really matter though because it was always cosy warm, especially in the sitting room which had a large fireplace and a big wooden chessboard which they took turns playing. Lucille showed off her cooking skills and made 'tarte aux pommes' or apple tart. After dinner, she would sit by the flames of the fire telling stories about her family and life in France. Babu curled up on the sofa next to her and kept her extra warm and snug.

When the last day came, the weather thankfully had improved, and the drive back was pleasant and restful. Nana had given Lucille a little box containing a pair of earrings as a little present to take home with her and the blog and video were mostly complete but for a few edits to complete on the journey home. The family all waved Lucille off at the airport as she met up with the rest of the French exchange group along with the other families. The girls promised to stay in touch. They had already agreed to meet in France the following year.

Chapter 8

The Grande Mosquée de Paris has a hidden jewel inside its doors. Escaping the busy crowds, it serves as a secret retreat away from the hustle and bustle of the city. Small glasses are filled to the brim with fresh mint tea that sit on the small silver trays with tiny pots of honey glistening in the sunlight. Birds flit about the small branches of the trees. Bertrand loved to spend whole afternoons just sitting in the gardens of the mosque. It was so tranquil for him and such a peaceful place.

Bertrand would often retrace his steps from where the bomb had hit many years before at the Metro at Porte de la Chapelle. He had lost his memory that fateful day and had been trying ever since to find out who he really was. He was told the exact location where it had happened, when he woke up in the hospital. The hospital staff explained that he had amnesia and since that time, he only ever remembered being in the hospital with no recollection of his life prior to that event.

In recent times, the doctor had advised that by possibly retracing his steps to the Metro, this could potentially trigger his memory recovery and life before the war. He would often be deep in thought, frustrated that his memory would not return and he could not recall his life before the bombing. He wished that he knew where he came from, what his real name was and who his family were and whether they were still alive. He did not show his feelings to his close family and the mystery surrounding who he was was something he tried to figure out on his own.

He took a long sip from the glass, which was cooling and refreshing, even though piping hot, and he dried his lips with his white handkerchief before putting it back into his pocket. He walked out from the mosque, into the street and hailed a taxi to be taken to the metro station at Porte de la Chapelle.

The yellow and brown autumnal leaves fluttered down before being swept up by the wind and circling down once more. The Metro was in sight and Bertrand looked fixedly towards the main sign trying to picture the angle in which he would have approached all those years ago. *I wonder which direction I was coming from?* he thought to himself and drew in a long breath of sharp air. Standing for some time, he looked at his old watch and remembered that he had better get back to the rail station. Happily, Bertrand had missed the rush hour, thus his journey was pleasant enough as he peered through the window of the train and looked out across the rooftops of Paris.

A week later, a phone call from his granddaughter saw Bertrand return to the city centre in Paris. He bought his usual mille-feuille pastry from his favourite bakery. It was a breezy day and the leaves swirled about the path. He met his granddaughter in the park. Taking her arm, they strolled along together.

'Papa, what have you been up to?' she asked, 'I see you have been eating your favourite cake!' she said wiping the cream from his cheek.

'Oh, just walking and thinking, my usual past time,' he replied. He had spent the summer at home in the house that he had shared with his late wife, Juliette. He had met Juliette shortly before the end of the war, and they had set up home outside of the city. He had assisted in the rebuilding of parts of Paris which had been devastated by the war. They had two grown-up children and he doted on his granddaughters. They walked arm in arm along the row of tall trees and beech hedges. Their scarves were placed high up to cover their mouths as the cool winds came in from the North. His granddaughter whistled a tune and merrily repeated it once again as they walked along avoiding small puddles in their stride.

They entered Le Petit Cadeau, a cosy restaurant that served hearty warm cuisine. They hung up their coats on the coat rail. They took a seat by the window and watched as a cellist began to play outside the main door of the restaurant.

'I haven't seen you in ages and you know how much I miss you.' Bertrand took his granddaughter's hand and held it tightly for a moment. He ordered French onion soup for two and they listened to the faint sounds of the music from outside. The soft red velvet cushions and clinking of glasses made for a pleasant atmosphere away from the chilly outdoors.

Bertrand's wife had sadly passed away some five years back and meetings with his granddaughter were always special times. She reminded him of his beautiful wife with her long curly golden hair and bright smile. As they sat and chatted, they felt warm in the familiar restaurant.

'Papa, I have made a film of my travels this summer. You know the girl that came to visit us? Well, I visited her and we had such a wonderful time!'

'Where did you go?' her grandfather asked.

'Well, we were based in Norwich which is a lovely city with a big colourful market and lots of great shopping and a castle and cathedral. There's the Norfolk Broads which is a man-made waterway in Norfolk where there's lots of sailing and motorboats so we sketched some of the boats and I saw an otter and a seal. It's a very picturesque place to visit. Lord Nelson, who led the Battle of Trafalgar, was from there.'

'Ah, I see you know your history,' he chuckled.

'The second week of the holiday, we drove up to a place in Cumbria which was a long way from any shops and stood on a hill. Sadly, it was freezing outside, and I caught a bit of a cold but there was a cat named Babu and he cuddled into me to keep me warm!' Bertrand smiled and ate his hearty soup, listening intently to every word. Looking out of the window he watched as a passer-by leant down and dropped some change into the cellist's cap. 'The young daughter played a cello just like that one. Have a look and see my photos.' She passed her iPad to him and he looked through the photos one at a time.

'Their Nana Rose never sat down for a moment; she was always on her feet! A busy bee's work is never done! This is what she said!'

Her grandfather stopped for a moment, took the hand-kerchief from his pocket and daubed his mouth. He remembered someone saying that to him before. The thought was fleeting. He looked at the photos and stopped at a picture of a grand house and again a picture flashed into his mind of a piano as if he were sitting opposite it. His granddaughter excused herself and went to the bathroom, while Bertrand continued to look through the photographs.

When she ambled back she hummed a tune under her breath and stood for a moment looking out across at the cellist. Sitting back down she looked deeply into her grand-father's eyes. Bertrand continued to whistle the tune quietly to himself and carried on although she had stopped.

'I whistle this tune myself in my head sometimes and wish I knew what it was called.'

'Oh yes that tune is what Emily, the sister of my pen friend played on her cello, I'm sure of it.' Scrambling for the video she took, she played it to him and he watched and listened. Once again he whistled it back and continued to whistle the tune, as if completing the piece when the video clip had stopped playing.

'Wait a second,' she said and texted her friend. 'I'm just finding out what that tune is.'

A response immediately came back saying, 'I don't know, I'll have to ask Emily. Give me a second.'

Reading out the text, it said, 'It was composed by Leni. In fact, it was written by my Great Uncle Leni before he died in the war. He never finished it completely but I love the tune!'

Another text was sent, 'Why are you asking?'

All these texts were read aloud by Lucille.

'Because my grandfather knows it.'

Their main course arrived and they both settled back to eating once again, putting the phone and the iPad down. Her grandfather looked deep in thought whilst eating and they sat in silence once again, listening to the cello music from outside. Wiping his mouth with a serviette, Bertrand again held his granddaughter's wrists gently but firmly. Tears welled up in his eyes.

'Lucille,' he spoke quietly. 'I believe that you may have discovered part of my past.'

Laying on the bed in Lizzie's bedroom, Emily had been reading the texts that had been coming in from Lucille. She looked wide-eyed at her sister, Lizzie. 'Because my grandfather knows it,' she said repeatedly. 'Why would he know it? How would he know the tune? No one knows it, do they?' she went on, puzzled.

'Oh Emily, I don't know about you but I'm going out and I need to get ready.'

Lizzie stood up and started rifling through her wardrobe, frantically trying to find an outfit to wear for going out. 'What about this one?'

Clearly finding a dress and the right shoes was going to take time, so Emily went back to her own room quietly slipping out of the door. She thought how strange it was that Lucille's grandfather could know this tune but then again maybe he got confused and mixed it up with another tune he already knew. She gave it little more thought just before picking up her cello for a short practice before dinner.

Chapter 9

After saying goodbye to Lucille at the train station, Bertrand walked home and sat straight down at his writing table. His wife had had some manuscript paper somewhere in the house and he found it amongst a pile of old papers. It was getting late but he did not think of the time or the late hour, just the music that was his composition. He started to write the entire piece for piano and cello, taking his time and not making any mistakes. A number of hours later, he yawned and stopped to reflect on the work he had completed. He was only part way through completing the score and there were many hours to be spent composing the entire piece. Tired, he knew he needed to rest so he lay down to slumber. He closed his eyes and soon fell into a deep sleep and began to dream.

In his dream, he was running about a meadow full of summer flowers with bees and butterflies hovering above the grasses. His sister giggled as they ran towards the big old house and into the arms of their mother. In the kitchen, he sat across from his sister pulling faces whilst eating jelly before playing music in the music room with his sister at the piano. Blue and white hues of light flashed into the dream leading out from the music room into the hall. The music notebook fleetingly came into view and a photographer who took photos of him with his cello. With a mix of colours, the dream changed from his youth to military school, where he was older now and sitting at a long table with officers at each side. He was being instructed about plans and responsibilities before finding himself sitting in a train surrounded by soldiers as it trundled towards its destination. A mist seemed to follow him as a smoky haze was surrounding him. He walked alone along streets and gutters as the colours turned to grey.

Chapter 10

Emily's cello teacher, Lotte, had two black cats, Bella and Mitsy, who curled around her ankles as she entered the house and purred as she waited in the adjoining room for her first cello lesson to start. Much like Nana Rose's home, Lotte had other pupils who came to the house and Emily waited patiently next door listening to the music until it was time for her lesson. A young girl about Lizzie's age was in the middle of her lesson playing Elgar's Cello Concerto, stopping in places followed by unrecognisable chatting in between. The velvet curtains and dense smell from the wooden furniture made for a relaxing mood and the perfect place to curl up with a book, Emily thought.

Lotte was Dutch but had lived in Norwich for many years. She was medium height with long black hair, a beaming smile and kind eyes. Lotte greeted Emily warmly when they met and she led her through to the music room that was to become Emily's weekly retreat for learning.

During that first cello lesson Lotte said, 'What a beautiful cello,' inspecting the cello closely and looking through to the sound board inside.

'This belonged to my Nana when she was a little girl,' Emily announced.

Lotte tried it out herself and played a beautiful tune on the instrument showing all her skill and making the cello come alive with the resonating sound that was produced. 'Do show me what you have been playing,' Lotte said, and so began Emily taking her bow and playing the little horn-pipe she had been practising at home.

'Your lessons will comprise of these technique books to develop your hand positions and intonation and we will use this G1-5 scale book, picking out pieces that you will be able to work through each week.' Lotte played through Emily's three chosen examination pieces from the Associated Board of the Royal Schools of Music (ABRSM) music books, all of differing genres and styles played on her own old cello. The small room echoed with sound. 'Every December I hold a music evening where all my pupils play music together sharing the pieces by performing them in an evening concert. Please come and perform with us!' Emily was so excited with the prospect of performing at a concert, especially the chance to be able to play alongside others. Emily so enjoyed her weekly lessons. Lotte's Dutch accent pronounced words very interestingly with soft lilting sounds, she thought. Emily, was so inspired by her teacher and could hardly wait to show her Nana her progress during her next visit to Cumbria.

Emily's routine was to practise for twenty-five minutes twice per day and when her father got home from work, he enjoyed listening to her playing most evenings. One day he popped his head into her bedroom and he asked if he could sit in the room to be able to watch her playing and she played all of her pieces to him.

'Wow, I can see you are a natural at this! You are really improving! Your determination to play and develop your skills is very impressive, your mother and I are very proud of you!'

Bruce was a kind and hard-working man who often arrived home late from his work as an engineer. No matter how tiring his day had been, he always seemed to find enough time to listen to Emily practice or sit with Lizzie if she ever needed help with her homework before the girls went off to bed.

Chapter 11

The next morning Bertrand awoke very early with his mind still racing. He sat down after breakfast in his armchair with his music manuscript papers in his hands and closed his eyes to recount and place the flood of memories that were coming back to him.

'My name is Leonard Peters,' he declared out loud.

Leni started to speak whole sentences in English. He remembered learning the cello and teaching his little sister when she was old enough and tall enough to be able to play the smaller cello. The emotions of joy and amazement were mixed with anticipation and he needed to take his time to process the memories that were so rapidly coming back to him. He looked at the framed photo of his wife as he lifted it from the small table beside his desk. For all those years he had lived not knowing who he truly was and he so wished that his late wife was there to share the good news. He looked around at the dusty room and out towards the French doors. There was no time to waste.

He booked a train ticket to Cumbria via London and pulled out his suitcase ready to pack from the wardrobe. He carefully placed, between his clothes, framed photographs of his wife, his two children and grandchildren. He neatly lay the music manuscript papers upon his packed clothes and closed up the suitcase. By ten o'clock he was already sitting on the train. He kept muttering to himself under his breath as he pronounced words in varying dialects to himself. He smiled as he recalled even his old Cumbrian accent which was returning back to him very strongly.

When he reached England, he thought back to his days training to be an agent of the Special Operations Executive and how he had been so rigorously tested on his command of dialects by people from a variety of regions. By using his talent for mimicry to imitate all manner of language and accents, he had passed all the observational exercises with flying colours.

He remembered the day that he was to leave for France, and the wish to tell his family all about what he had been posted to do but his family had no idea that he was embarking on a secret intelligence mission. He boarded the train that day knowing just how difficult the mission would be and the likely possibility that he would never return. With mixed feelings of pride and apprehension, he had held his sister close knowing how much she adored and would miss him.

As the train emerged from the Channel Tunnel he was back in England. Changing trains, he waited patiently at St Pancras Station for his connection before taking a window seat and settling to read. He could not resist trying out his English accents again and took on a Liverpool accent and later a London Cockney accent to test whether he still had a command of dialects. He discussed the weather and how long the journey would take, with a lady who sat opposite to him and she did not appear at all to question whether he was French or English. He supposed that she would have asked him had she queried the tone and inflections and chuckled quietly to himself. Opening a book and putting on his reading glasses, he read a little before drifting off into a long snooze.

When he awoke, he recognised the differing and altering countryside as the train travelled northwards and tried to recall station names and whether he remembered what they used to look like.

When he finally reached Cumbria, the strong feeling of homecoming surprised him. The rich wide-open spaces with dry stone walling, crows in the trees and fells in the distance felt very familiar to him. He was elated knowing that the years searching for his past were almost over. Fleetingly he remembered hiking up Blencathra with his friends in his younger days but could not recall the names of his friends. Hikers got on and got off the train in their hiking gear and cyclists stood patiently at station gates waiting for train connections. He opened the window to smell the fresh air of the fells and longed to hear the sound of the curlew again and the many other birds he used to see and hear in the garden and surrounding countryside.

He thought about his cello and about his music notebook with so many of his compositions and felt a sense of wonderment that both had been kept for all these years. He closed his eyes and pictured the house, with its entrance hall, stained glass window of a tiny bird on the wide front wooden door, of the Aga in the kitchen and the log fire in the sitting room. He pictured his old bedroom and the bathroom and the oak tree outside. He had wondered whether he should have contacted his sister Rose before leaving Paris. However, he had decided that the emotions of the reunion would be best shared in person. His journey was to end the way that it had started; by hugging his sister.

Slowly his excitement could hardly be contained but he gave little away to the surrounding commuters and travelers who were going about their day. Finally, the train stopped in Carlisle and he walked to the front steps of the station. He stood awhile with his suitcase and looked about trying to remember the station. He had taken a hotel room in the city that night and bought a huge bunch of flowers for his sister for the following day. The taxi driver did not have a clue where the house was but knew the nearest village. Leni hoped that as he neared the little village, he would remember exactly how to find the old house.

As the car sped along the tiny roads and mud splattered lanes, he passed an old red tractor and a flock of sheep on the road. Rolling down the window he felt right at home amid the smells of the countryside.

'Nice flowers you have there,' the taxi driver said. 'Are you visiting a friend?'

'Indeed I am,' Leni confirmed catching the taxi driver's eye in the mirror.

For the remainder of the journey, Leni sat in silence and his mind wandered. Leni's memory had more or less come back to him except for the period he spent in Paris just before the bomb blast. In the hospital, he was told the full story of the bombing when he had first entered the Metro. During his recovery in the ward, a young French woman had left flowers by his bedside and when he was able to open his eyes and begin the process of healing, the lady thanked him and explained that the time he had entered the Metro and went down the steps there had been a number of shudders and bombings nearby and she had rushed, liked many others, and stumbled hurting her ankle. He had taken off his thick coat to shelter and assist her. When the bomb hit and the shrapnel had gone into his chest and thigh, she had remained in the most part unscathed and believed this was due to the protection of his body and the thickness of the reefer jacket he had sheltered her with.

Her kindness turned to friendship and in time they fell in love. They married after the war and went on to have two children. Leni had worked in the offices that were in charge of rebuilding the city following the devastation from the allied bombings. He was quick to learn and his bright intellect was soon acknowledged as he took up his post of District Planner.

The taxi driver pulled up at the village square. As if it were yesterday, Leni remembered exactly the directions from the village and directed the driver to the foot of the paddock at the old house. Stepping out, he touched the stone wall and knew that he was home. He walked slowly hearing the faint sound of a Bach prelude being played on the piano in the distance. A white cat leisurely walked towards him and caressed his leg as he sat for a moment on the wall savouring the sight of the big old house with its dark brown reddish sandstone. He walked to the side gate and slowly past the apple trees which were hanging low, laden with fruit. He could smell the rich smells from the herb garden. He took his time and entered the door, gazing at the stained glass that he knew so well. Hesitating slightly he did not quite know how to signal his arrival so he simply rang the little bell and retreated back from the front step.

His mind flashed back to when he was twenty, standing in the doorway tall and handsome and awaiting his sister to come running out to hug him. He took a deep breath. He knew the door would be open but waited for some time. The loud piano music continued, and he wondered whether his sister could have heard the bell. He stepped forward and gently pushed open the door and waited before ringing the bell once again. The piano stopped and he heard the familiar sound of the music door opening. Rose stepped out into the hall.

As Rose stood for a moment, squinting her eyes towards the light, she looked toward the figure silhouetted in the doorway who was holding a huge bouquet of flowers.

'Perhaps a little later than expected my dear Rosie,' Leni said calmly. Rose knew it was her brother standing there the moment she had stepped into the hall and she rushed towards him. She hugged him tightly and they both wept for joy in disbelief. 'I knew you would come back,' Rose cried out. 'I never gave up hope.'

Babu took to his seat and both Rose and Leni sat together beside the warm Aga talking for many hours into the night and for many days thereafter until they had completely caught up on each other's lives.

Chapter 12

Lucille cycled round to her grandfather's house taking some freshly prepared chicken flan cooked by her mother in the basket at the front of her bicycle. She approached the door and after knocking a number of times noticed that her grandfather was not at home. She found the front door key under a plant pot at the back of the house in its secret location next to a plum tree. Opening the door, some post from the letter box fell to the floor unopened. She called out, searched the kitchen and the living room and then ran up the stairs and into his bedroom. The bed was neatly made, and an envelope lay on the top blanket with Lucille's name written clearly in her grandfather's handwriting.

She opened it and saw a cryptic code in her grandfather's hand which she needed to break in order to understand the letter. She loved her grandfather's coding which had become a game between the two over the years. This one looked like an alphabet shift and Lucille looked for cribs within the text which would help her break the code.

Cribs are common phrases or words that help establish the secret of the code. This was how the British codebreakers deciphered the coded messages generated by the Enigma Machine at Bletchley Park which was used by the Germans during the Second World War. Curiously, the only clue she had was that her grandfather had recently produced codes for her that were written in English and not French so with that in mind she smiled, laid back on the bed and looked to break the secret code.

She first looked for single letter words and there were only two her grandfather had told her to look for if ever translating an English code. The one letter words 'i' and 'a'. With this she could see the shift in the alphabet used in the code. Cleverly, her grandfather had not signed his name in code at the end of the letter as this would have been the easiest of cribs to use. The letter read as follows:

"n fr xt ymfspkzq ymfy dtz mfaj wjrnsiji rj tk rd ufxy fsi gwtzlmy fqq rd rjrtwnjx kqttinsl gfhp yt rj. n fr sty xzwj nk dtz mfaj knlzwji ymnx tzy djy gzy qneenj, dtzw ujs kwnjsi, mfx f sfsf bmt nx fhyzfqqd rd xnxyjw! jrnqd uqfdx rd tqi hjqqt n knwxy qjfwsji ts fsi ymj qnyyqj unjhj dtz bmnxyqji fsi pstb xt bjqq nx rd tbs htrutxnynts. n htrutxji ny rtwj ymfs ktwyd djfwx flt! rd rjrtwnjx fwj fqq kqtbnsl gfhp fsi n htzqi sty bfny tsj rtrjsy qtsljw yt ywfajq gfhp yt rd xnxyjw ns hzrgwnf xt n yttp f ywfns. uqjfxj htsyfhy jrnqd fsi qneenj fsi xjsi ts tzw wjlfwix! dtz bnqq rtxy uwtgfgqd mfaj wjfi ymnx gd ymj ynrj n bnqq mfaj fwwnaji ymjwj. n it mtuj yt xjj dtz xtts. uqjfxj bfyjw rd uqfsyx fsi ymj qjrts ajw-gjsf ns ymj xnyynsl wttr! lnaj rd qtaj yt dtzw ufwjsyx. rd wjfq sfrj nx ufuf qjsn"*

---

* Lucille's translated transcript of the puzzle can be found at the back of the book

Chapter 13

Leni was quite moved hearing all the stories of Rose's life. His sister had not changed one bit and radiated the same warm glow and twinkle in her eye that she had always had. Rose asked lots of questions and was fascinated to hear that he had been selected by the British government as part of a secret intelligence agency called the Special Operations Executive. As one of the SOE's spies in France, he needed to blend in as a local Frenchman. The SOE excelled at blending their officers into communities. The organisation even employed seamstresses and tailors to create bespoke clothing common to the area the officers were assigned to.

Leni showed Rose the photos of his wife and children and talked about the frustrations he had had since the bombing to find out his true identity. Never once did he suspect that he was British but since his memory had returned, he was astounded at his ability to go back to speaking English with such fluency.

On the third day, Rose walked into the sitting room with Leni's old music notebooks in her hand. 'I think it is time we finished the music which brought us together again,' Rose said, smiling.

Leni made a fire and the siblings looked through the old paper pages together, examining each of the pieces. Laying her hand on his they set about planning how they would finalise the music and spent the afternoon at the piano playing through the original compositions.

Getting the cello out of its case was hugely moving for Leni. It had recently been tuned and was ready to be played. Leni did not know whether he would be able to remember how to play it but as soon as he took a seat and placed the bow onto the four strings he relished playing each of the open strings and was able to play fluently, following the music quite easily. 'Just like riding a bike,' he said. 'You never forget.'

Taking to the writing table with his new manuscript notebook, with the original music manuscript laid out in front of him, Leni continued composing the music with the intention of completing the whole work. He closed his eyes allowing the music to flow into his mind and gradually completed the score. He decided to revise all the music pieces in the book and thought that it would be a lovely gift to have the music published one day. Excited by the prospect, Leni worked daily on his music compositions, taking short breaks in the garden to reflect and rest as Rose busied herself about the house.

Chapter 14

Upon breaking the code, Lucille cycled home and told her parents the whole story. That evening, Lucille's father rang the Peters family and it was agreed that both families would travel to Rose and Leni to spend Christmas together. The plan was to keep the visit secret from Emily and Lizzie. Leni and Rose had insisted that they wanted to surprise Emily and make her Christmas extra special.

'Papa Bertrand or should I now call you Leni,' Lucille laughed, 'I have contacted Lizzie and Emily to say 'hello' but I have not told them about you getting your memory back nor who you actually are. This means that they still don't know your true identity! I've told Mum and Dad and they were fine with this. Are you okay too?'

'Absolutely,' Leni said, 'this will be the best Christmas present for everyone and what a treat for Emily. If it wasn't for her love of my melody and playing the cello well, maybe my memory would never have come back!'

Leni looked at his old leather satchel and opened his new finished music manuscripts. All the pieces were now complete before Christmas. Rose and Leni practised through each of the music pieces together in the music room with the little burner flames keeping them warm in the wintery climate.

Christmas plans were well underway. Having the whole

family to stay with Emily, Lizzie, their Mum and Dad, Lucille and her parents, this would be quite an occasion.

Leni brought in the Christmas tree, and after some time of getting it to stand straight and turning it to the best orientation, they delighted at putting the lights up and hanging the old decorations. Old George the butcher delivered the turkey and ham to the house; he had single-handedly told almost the entire village about Leni's return and it felt like nearly all of the villagers had visited the house over the past weeks to welcome him home and take the opportunity to savour Rose's renowned baking and chutneys. Even the local Chronicle sent a reporter round to write an article which became front page local news the following week. News spread fast and it was not long before the national newspapers and broadcasters were in contact wanting to run the story. Leni and Rose were struck with the interest in their story and agreed to meet with journalists early in the New Year.

The house was set with holly, ivy and a piece of mistletoe that hung above the main door to welcome each visitor. Lucille and her parents were the first family to arrive and had been very excited to travel over to Cumbria for the first time. They took a flight to Manchester and travelled on the train for the remaining part of the journey.

There were many presents under the tree and Rose was so happy to have the house full of people at Christmas. Lucille brought her flute from France and it wasn't long before there was music playing all over the house. Lucille's parents also played instruments and had brought their clarinet and violin along. Lucille and her mother looked through the bookshelves together and found lots of trios, quartets and duets which were played joyously together. That night the family settled in front of the fire to plan how they were going to surprise Emily and Lizzie. They were due to arrive in the car the following day and the forecast was for heavy snow to start falling late in the afternoon, so they hoped they would miss the storms on their way up.

The following day, the house was quiet as the families lay in bed a little longer than usual. Nana Rose was first up and made fresh bread, kneading the dough and preparing the ingredients ready for the Christmas feasts ahead. Babu yawned and snuggled on his favourite chair and Rose caught a glimpse of the old photo of her dear brother Leni from all those years ago. Somehow, she had always known in her heart that her brother was still alive and that he would come back home and as she stood reminiscing, a silent tear ran down her cheek. Leni came into the kitchen and put on some Duke Ellington jazz music from the 1940s. He took Rose is his arms and the two danced around the kitchen floor, giggling together.

Lucille was the next to come down for some breakfast and Leni reached out to her, took her arm and the three glided across the floor.

Lucille had hardly slept through the night as she masterminded Emily's arrival and the big surprise. She sat down for her breakfast and proceeded to tell them both about her idea.

'We shall practise this morning playing some of the music together and when you go to the door and welcome the family, they will walk through to the sitting room, sit down for some tea and Papa Leni can start to play alongside Great Aunt Rose,' she went on, 'they will hear this music and when they come in, the penny will drop! You must all hide in the sitting room because they will all walk round from the car and I would hope that they don't look in because they will see Papa Leni!' With the plan in place the family rehearsed their pieces together ready for the big surprise.

The house was abuzz with activity. As the family practised various music pieces, Rose prepared the Christmas Eve lunch and sang along to the various classical and Christmas music being rehearsed. A text came in at midday from Emily letting her know that they were now in Penrith and it would not be long before their arrival. Rose looked outside into the garden hopeful that they would arrive before the storm started. Before long, away in the distance, the car could be seen, and it rumbled and jolted slowly along and up the hill.

When the car stopped and the hand brake went on, little snowflakes began to flutter about the car and Emily jumped out. Babu meowed from the side of the house and came bounding towards them as they opened the little gate. Emily bent down to pick him up in her arms and was struck by the distinct sound of a cello and piano playing from the house. She stood up and thought she was hearing the distinct melody of her Great Uncle Leni's piece. The music then stopped abruptly.

'Right everyone,' Bruce said, 'Let's get in out of this snow and I'll empty the car later.'

Putting Babu down, Emily picked up her rucksack and her cello and dashed ahead of the others. 'Nana, we're here,' she called out. When she reached the front door, she tried to push it open but the door was locked.

Her parents arrived at the door and Mary said, 'Knock three times Emily.' Emily gave a puzzled look to her mum and reached up to the door knocker.

The large wooden door opened slowly and Lucille, to Emily's surprise, was standing dressed in a bright red hooded cape. Putting her finger to her lips Lucille requested silence. As they stepped inside, Lucille kissed each one of them on both cheeks under the mistletoe. The hallway was lined on both sides with candles leading to the music room at the far end. Lizzie and Emily looked at each other with confused expressions on their faces and followed Lucille in a graceful procession towards the music room.

On the music room door hung the old photograph of Emily's Great Uncle Leni. Gathered together, the girls stood back gazing at the photograph for a moment wondering what all these dramatics were about. Lucille graciously gestured the family inside.

Nana Rose was at the piano next to an elderly man who

was sitting beside her with his cello. The piano began to play the introduction and the family were transfixed. Emily knew the piece very well and when the cellist started to play, Emily's jaw dropped in the realisation that her Great Uncle Leni was sitting before her with his leather satchel at his feet.

Chapter 15

Emily awoke early Christmas morning. She opened the curtains, revealing a winter wonderland outside. The snow had stopped falling and a white blanket covered the landscape and trees. She headed downstairs in her pyjamas to the kitchen where Nana Rose had made a huge pot of porridge and her Great Uncle Leni got a bowl and a spoon for her.

'Did you sleep well, Emily?' Leni asked.

'Like a log,' Emily replied.

'Like a yule log,' her Nana Rose giggled.

The three sat down together and Leni took the hands of both Rose and Emily. 'Rose and I would like to thank you from the bottom of our hearts for persevering in your wish to play the cello. Your desire to play and your inquisitive nature brought about bringing the cellos down from the attic which gave my dear Rose the courage to play my music, even though it brought back such difficult memories. In so doing, she rekindled what is so important in our lives, that we should not fear our memories but embrace our dreams. If I had not heard my music being played, I too would never have discovered who I am and the triggering of all my memories returning back to me.'

Leni had a very special surprise for Emily on Christmas Day. She sat down on her cello chair and showed Leni one of her pieces. He smiled before he handed her a rather large wrapped present. Not sure whether to open the present or wait for her parents to come downstairs, he gestured for her to go ahead and open it.

Inside was a lovely leather satchel with the initials, 'E.P.' inscribed on the front.

Emily opened the brand new satchel and inside was a notebook filled with music.

In the opening dedication she read out loud: 'To Emily, A remarkable cellist who will be forever making memories for others.'

Chapter 16

Some years later, The Bridgewater Hall was packed full of people for the premiere of the cello concerto performance. 'Bravo!' Bravo! The entire concert hall rose to their feet to rapturous applause at the end. The solo cellist took her bow and the audience roared in appreciation. As the applause continued, the cellist looked down towards the front row gesturing to a frail elderly gentleman to stand up from his seat and turn to face the audience. As the composer slowly stood up, helped by the arm of his sister Rose at his side, he looked up at Emily, blew her a little kiss and turned towards the audience to take his bow.

Secret code for Leni's letter:

'I am so thankful that you have reminded me of my past and brought all my memories flooding back to me. I am not sure if you have figured this out yet but Lizzie, your pen friend, has a Nana who is actually my sister! Emily plays my old cello I first learned on and the little piece you whistled and know so well is my own composition. I composed it more than forty years ago! My memories are all flowing back and I could not wait one moment longer to travel back to my sister in Cumbria so I took a train. Please contact Emily and Lizzie and send on our regards! You will most probably have read this by the time I will have arrived there. I do hope to see you soon. Please water my plants and the lemon verbena in the sitting room! Give my love to your parents. My real name is Papa Leni.'

Lightning Source UK Ltd.
Milton Keynes UK
UKHW040727060220
358272UK00002B/394